The name Star Bright Books and the Star Bright Books logo are registered trademarks of Star Bright Books, Inc. Please visit: www.starbrightbooks.com. For bulk orders, please email: orders@starbrightbooks.com, or call customer service at: (617) 354-1300.

Hardcover ISBN-13: 978-1-59572-845-6
Paperback ISBN-13: 978-1-59572-846-3
Star Bright Books / MA / 00106190
Printed in China / Toppan / 9 8 7 6 5 4 3 2 1

Printed on paper from sustainable forests.

Library of Congress Cataloging-in-Publication Data

Names: Gorbachev, Valeri, author, illustrator.
Title: Pinky's fair day / by Valeri Gorbachev.
Description: [Cambridge], MA : Star Bright Books, [2019] | Summary: Pinky the pig wants to be a good helper, like the Hedgehog Brothers, but although he tries his best, he fails to help his neighbors get ready for the fair.
Identifiers: LCCN 2018055123| ISBN 9781595728456 (hardback) | ISBN 9781595728463 (pbk.)
Subjects: | CYAC: Helpfulness--Fiction. | Neighbors--Fiction. | Robbers and outlaws--Fiction.
Classification: LCC PZ7.G6475 Pg 2019 | DDC [E]--dc23
LC record available at https://lccn.loc.gov/2018055123

:ri Gorbachev

Pinky's Fair Day

STAR BRIGHT BOOKS
CAMBRIDGE MASSACHUSETTS

The big county fair was coming to town! Pinky hurried over to watch his neighbors get ready for it.

When he got there, he ran into the Hedgehog brothers.

"What are you so happy about, little Hedgehogs?" he asked.

"We did such a good job painting the fence for Mrs. Raccoon. She called us great helpers!" they said.

"Big deal!" said Pinky. "If I wanted, everyone would call me a great helper, too!"

Then Pinky saw Mrs. Sheep hanging the decorations.

"Mrs. Sheep, would you call me a great helper if I helped you with your work?" he asked.

"Sure!" Mrs. Sheep replied. "Can you please hand me those little flags?"

"I'll get this done in a jiffy!" cried Pinky.
"Oh no, help! I am tangled in the flags!"

"Hmm, I think you are not a very good helper, Pinky," Mrs. Sheep said as she untangled Pinky from the little flags. "I don't need help like *this*."

Pinky ran to Mr. Goat's carpenter shop to see if he needed any help.

"Mr. Goat, will you call me a great helper if I help you with your work?" he asked.

"Sure," said Mr. Goat. "There is so much work to do with the fair coming to town."

"Oh, I love these rocking chairs you made for the fair!"
Pinky squealed.

"I love rocking in them. You're a great craftsman, Mr. Goat!"

"But you are not a great helper, Pinky," Mr. Goat said. "Instead of helping me, you're just rocking in the chairs!"

"Sorry!" said Pinky. "I just love to rock!"

Pinky ran out to see if someone else would thank him for his help.

"Mr. Boar, will you call me a great helper if I help you with your work?" asked Pinky.

"Sure," Mr. Boar replied. "You see all those pots I made for the fair? If you can load them on to my cart, you would really be helping me out."

"This will take no time at all.
I can do it easily!" Pinky boasted.
"Be careful!" called Mr. Boar.
"I will!" said Pinky.

"Oops!"

"Look what you have done!" scolded Mr. Boar. "There is nothing left of my pots but broken pieces. I don't need your help any more!"

"Sorry!" said Pinky. "I tried my best!"

Pinky ran to see if someone else would thank
him for his help.

"Hey, Pinky! Why don't you help us?" called
Mrs. Crow. "Mrs. Owl and I have so many things to
do. We are in a hurry to get to the fair. Maybe you
can sweep the floor while we bake the dumplings."

"Okay!" said Pinky. "But will you call me a great
helper if I work well?"

"Of course we will!" Mrs. Crow said. "Just get to work!"

"I will be done in a jiffy!" said Pinky.

"AAH-CHOO!!!" sneezed Mrs, Crow and Mrs. Owl.

"Look at all the dust you spun up!" Mrs. Crow exclaimed. "We don't need your help any more!"

"Sorry!" said Pinky. "I tried my best!"

"Nobody likes my help!" Pinky said sadly.
"No one calls me a great helper. Nobody
needs me . . ."

"*We* need your help, Pinky!" called two
strangers, Cat and Dog. "We will call you a
great helper!"

"Really?" Pinky asked excitedly. "What do
you want me to do?"

"We will show you. We will teach you!" said Cat.
"Just follow our lead."
    "Hey!" Pinky yelled. "What are you doing?!"

"We are just picking some apples," said Dog. "They look so delicious. We will make a fortune selling them at the fair!"

"But they are not yours!" Pinky exclaimed. "I don't want to be your helper! And look—I've torn my pants! Now what will I do?"

"Don't worry," said Cat. "We will take care of it. Look, there are lots of clothes in that wagon!"

And before Pinky could say anything, Cat and Dog
jumped in front of the Traveling Theater wagon.
    "Hand over your clothes!" they demanded.
    "Hey!" yelled Pinky. "What are you doing? Stop
that at once! Help! Somebody help! They are
robbing the puppet wagon!"

"Quick, let's get out of here!" shouted Dog.
"That ungrateful pig is going to ruin us!"
And Cat and Dog quickly ran away.

"I will help you now!" Pinky cried as he freed the puppeteers.

"Thank you for your help, Pinky!" said the puppet master. "You saved us from those terrible robbers!"

"Does this mean I am a great helper?" asked Pinky.

"Sure, of course you are!" said the puppet master.

"Wow!" exclaimed Pinky. "I can't wait to tell the Hedgehog brothers about this! I will hurry up and find them!"

He looked all over the fair for his little friends, but they were nowhere to be found.

Then Pinky saw Mrs. Raccoon doing laundry.

"Have you seen my friends, the Hedgehog brothers?" he asked.

"They are in the meadow hanging clean sheets out to dry," said Mrs. Raccoon. "They are great helpers."

"I can carry some of the sheets to the meadow!" Pinky offered.

Before Mrs. Raccoon had a chance to thank him, Pinky ran to the meadow.

"Hey, little Hedgehogs!" Pinky cried. "I am happy! The puppet master for the Traveling Theater called me a great helper! I saved the puppeteers from terrible robbers."

"Wow!" said the little Hedgehogs. "You are a true hero and a great helper, Pinky! How did you do it?"

"I just tried my best!" said Pinky.